Dear Parent:

We're happy to have you and your children part of the I Can Read family.

What recommends this beginning reading series is the wide range of books it offers: funny tales, animal stories, mysteries, historical fiction, poetry. With each successive shipment, you will be building an outstanding library of books.

Some of the best known writers and illustrators of children's books have contributed stories to the I Can Read canon. This book is no exception. Written by renowned author Russell Hoban and his wife Lillian Hoban, they have adapted their popular character, Frances (the badger) for the I Can Read format. (You may remember their book, *Bedtime for Frances.*)

In this book, Frances learns not to be duped by her little friend Thelma, so fiercely determined to own her own blue-flowered tea set. Frances learns to share, and learns, when it is important, to hold her own, too. Lillian Hoban's illustrations are endearing and just right.

Sincerely,

Fritz J. Luecke

Fritz J. Luecke
Editorial Director
Weekly Reader Book Club

An I Can Read Book®

A BARGAIN FOR FRANCES

by RUSSELL HOBAN
Pictures by LILLIAN HOBAN

HarperCollins*Publishers*

This book is a presentation of Newfield Publications, Inc.
Newfield Publications offers book clubs for children
from preschool through high school. For further
information write to: **Newfield Publications, Inc.,**
4343 Equity Drive, Columbus, Ohio 43228.

Published by arrangement with HarperCollins Publishers.
Newfield Publications is a federally registered trademark of
Newfield Publications, Inc.
I Can Read Book is a registered trademark of
HarperCollins Publishers.

A BARGAIN FOR FRANCES
Text copyright © 1970 by Russell C. Hoban
Pictures copyright © 1970 by Lillian Hoban

Library of Congress Catalog Card Number: 70-85033

For Phoebe, Brom, Esmé, and Julia

It was a fine summer day,

and after breakfast Frances said,

"I am going to play with Thelma."

"Be careful," said Mother.

7

"Why do I have to be careful?"
said Frances.

"Remember the last time?" said Mother.

"Which time was that?" said Frances.

"That was the time you played catch

with Thelma's new boomerang,"
said Mother. "Thelma did
all the throwing, and you came home
with lumps on your head."
"I remember that time now,"
said Frances.

"And do you remember the other time
last winter?" said Mother.
"I remember that time too,"
said Frances.

"That was the first time

there was ice on the pond.

Thelma wanted to go skating,

and she told me

to try the ice first."

"Who came home wet?" said Mother.

"You or Thelma?"

"I came home wet," said Frances.

"Yes," said Mother.

"That is why I say be careful.

Because when you play with Thelma

you always get the worst of it."

"Well," said Frances, "this time

I do not have to be careful.

We are not playing with boomerangs.

We are not skating.

We are having a tea party,

and we are making a mud cake."

"Be careful anyhow," said Mother.

"All right," said Frances.

Frances took her dolls
to Thelma's house.
She took her alligator doll
and her elephant doll.
She took her snake doll
and her teddy bear too.

As Frances walked to Thelma's house
she sang:

Alligators, bears and me
Are very fond of drinking tea.
The elephant and the wiggly snake
Are happy when they eat their cake.

Frances and Thelma made a mud cake.

They put daisies on it for frosting.

Then Thelma got out her dolls

and her tea set.

"I am saving up

for a tea set," said Frances.

"I am saving all my allowances."

"This is the best kind to get,"

said Thelma. "It is plastic,

and it has red flowers on it."

17

"That is not the kind I want,"
said Frances.
"I want a real china tea set
with pictures on it in blue.
The tea set I want has trees
and birds and a Chinese house
and a fence and a boat
and people walking on a bridge.
I used to have
that kind of tea set.
But all I have now
is part of the teapot.
The rest of it is broken."

"That is why that kind

of tea set is no good,"

said Thelma. "The cups break

and the saucers break

and the teapot and cream pitcher

and sugar bowl break,

and then the set is all gone.

My tea set has red flowers,

and it does not break

unless you step on it."

"Well," said Frances, "I am saving up

for the other kind."

"How much have you saved up?"

said Thelma.

"Two dollars and seventeen cents,"

said Frances.

"How much does the tea set cost?"

said Thelma.

"I don't know," said Frances.

"I am sure they cost a lot,"

said Thelma.

"It will take you a long time

to save up all that money."

"I know," said Frances, "and I wish

I had a tea set now."

"Maybe I will sell you mine,"

said Thelma.

"I don't want yours," said Frances.

"I want a real china one

with pictures on it in blue."

"I don't think
they make them anymore,"
said Thelma. "I know another girl
who saved up for that tea set.
Her mother went to every store
and could not find one.

Then that girl lost

some of her money

and spent the rest on candy.

She never got the tea set.

That is what happens.

A lot of girls

never do get tea sets.

So maybe you won't get one."

"If I buy yours, I will

have a tea set," said Frances.

26

"You said you didn't want it,"

said Thelma. "And anyhow,

I don't want to sell it now."

"Why not?" said Frances.

"Well," said Thelma,

"it is a very good tea set.

It is plastic that does not break.

It has pretty red flowers on it.

It has all the cups and saucers.

It has the sugar bowl

and the cream pitcher and the teapot.

It is almost new, and I think

it cost a lot of money."

"I have two dollars

and seventeen cents," said Frances.

"That's a lot of money."

"I don't know," said Thelma.

"If I sell you my tea set,

then I won't have one anymore."

"We can have tea parties

at my house then," said Frances.

"And you can use the money

for a new doll."

"Well, maybe," said Thelma.

"Do you have your money with you?"

"I'll run home for it," said Frances.

"All right," said Thelma.

"I will think about it

while you run home for your money."

Frances ran home for her money.

When she came back, Thelma said,

"I will sell you my tea set."

Frances gave Thelma her money.

Thelma gave Frances her tea set.

"No backsies on this," said Thelma.

"All right," said Frances.

"No backsies."

Frances went home with her tea set

and her dolls, and she sang:

A plastic pot can pour the tea

For my dolls and friends and me

Just as well as china.

Red is just as good as blue.

Plastic cups are all right too,

Just as good as china.

When Frances got home,

she showed the tea set

to her little sister Gloria.

"That is a very ugly tea set,"

said Gloria.

"What's the matter with it?"

said Frances.

"It's ugly," said Gloria.

"It's a nice tea set," said Frances.

"It's plastic," said Gloria.

"It has red flowers. It's ugly.

I like the china kind

with the pictures all in blue."

"You can't get that kind anymore,"
said Frances.

"They don't have them in the stores."

"Yes, they do," said Gloria.

"They have them now
at the candy store. My friend Ida
got one yesterday, and she showed it
to Thelma. So Thelma knows
they have them at the candy store.
They cost two dollars
and seven cents."

Frances walked slowly
to the candy store.

She looked inside,
and there was Thelma.

37

Thelma gave the storekeeper her money.

The storekeeper gave Thelma

a china tea set

with pictures all in blue.

Thelma did not see Frances

as Frances walked away.

Frances sang a little song
as she walked away:

Now that plastic's what I've got,

Backsies are what there is not.

Mother told me to be careful,

But Thelma better be bewareful.

39

Frances thought about no backsies

all the way home.

When she got home she put

a penny in the plastic sugar bowl

of her tea set.

Then she called Thelma

on the telephone.

"Hello," said Thelma.

"Hello," said Frances.

"This is Frances."

"Remember," said Thelma,

"no backsies."

"I remember," said Frances.

"But are you sure

you really want no backsies?"

"Sure I'm sure," said Thelma.

"You mean I never have to give back the tea set?" said Frances.

"That's right," said Thelma.

"You can keep the tea set."

"Can I keep what is in the sugar bowl too?" said Frances.

"What is in the sugar bowl?" said Thelma.

"Never mind," said Frances.

"No backsies. Good-bye."

Frances hung up.

Frances waited for the telephone
to ring, and when it rang
she said, "Hello."
"Hello," said Thelma.
"This is Thelma."
"I know," said Frances.

"I just remembered," said Thelma,

"I think I had something

in the sugar bowl.

I think it was a ring.

Did you find a ring?"

"No," said Frances. "And I don't have

to tell you what is in the sugar bowl

because you said no backsies."

"Well," said Thelma,

"I just remembered

that I put some money

in the sugar bowl one time.

I think it was some birthday money.

I think it was two dollars,

or maybe it was five dollars.

Did you find money?"

"You said no backsies," said Frances.

"So I don't have to tell you.

I don't have to say how much money

is in the sugar bowl."

"Well," said Thelma, "it is my money,

and I want it."

"Do you want backsies?" said Frances.

"Do you want your tea set back
and you will give my money back?"
"I can't," said Thelma,
"because I used the money
for a new tea set.
There is only a dime left over.
I will give you
the new tea set and the dime.
The new tea set is
the china kind you want.
It has pictures all in blue."
"You said they don't make that kind
anymore," said Frances.

"This one was very hard to find,"
said Thelma. "And I think it was
the very last one in the store."
"All right," said Frances.
"Bring it over."

Thelma brought over the china tea set
and the dime, and Frances gave back
the plastic tea set.

Then Thelma took the lid
off the sugar bowl
and saw the penny.

"That is not a very nice trick
to play on a friend," said Thelma.

"No," said Frances, "it is not.
And that was not a nice trick
you played on me
when you sold me your tea set."

"Well," said Thelma, "from now on
I will have to be careful
when I play with you."

"Being careful is not as much fun
as being friends," said Frances.
"Do you want to be careful,
or do you want to be friends?"

"I want to be friends," said Thelma.

"All right," said Frances.

"Then I will give you

halfies on the dime."

Frances and Thelma went
to the candy store with the dime.
Frances bought bubble gum,
and Thelma bought Life Savers.

Then they went back to Frances's house
to skip rope. Gloria came out
to turn the rope and skip too.

"You and Gloria can skip first,"
said Frances to Thelma.
"I will go last."

Thelma skipped first, then Gloria.

Then Frances skipped, and she sang:

One for plastic, two for china,

Three for yours and four for mine-a,

Five for tea and six for cakes,

Seven for elephants, eight for snakes,

Nine's a trip to the candy store,

Then comes ten and ten skips more:

Backsies one, backsies two,

Backsies are no fun to do.

Careful once, careful twice,

Being careful isn't nice.

Being friends is better.

Then Frances and Thelma

shared their bubble gum

and Life Savers with Gloria.